Rina's Rainy Day

A Gam Zu L'Tova Story

by Chani Altein • illustrated by Jerry Blackman

∽ ∽ ∽

Rina's Rainy Day
A Gam Zu L'Tova Story

To my husband for all of his support C.A.

• • •

To Heidi, for all her love and support J.B

• • •

First Edition – Adar 5768 / March 2008
Second Impression – Tishrei 5774 / October 2013
Third Impression – Elul 5777 / September 2017
Copyright © 2008 by HACHAI PUBLISHING
ALL RIGHTS RESERVED

Editor: D.L. Rosenfeld
Managing Editor: Yossi Leverton
Layout: Moshe Cohen

No part of this publication may be translated, reproduced, stored in a retrieval system, adapted or transmitted in any form or by any means, electronic, mechanical, photocopying, recording, or otherwise, without permission in writing from the copyright holder.

ISBN 13: 978-1-929628-39-1
ISBN 10: 1-929628-39-0
LCCN: 2007934552

HACHAI PUBLISHING
Brooklyn, New York
Tel: 718-633-0100 Fax: 718-633-0103
www.hachai.com info@hachai.com

Printed in China

Glossary
Gam zu l'tova - "This, too, is for the good."
Hashem - G-d
Ima - Mother
Mitzvos - Commandments, Good deeds

At the edge of some woods stood a house, small and sweet,
Painted light yellow, it looked nice and neat.

In it lived Rina, whom you'd recognize
By her red curls, her freckles, and dancing green eyes.

One day Rina said,
"This morning's so pretty,
The weather's just right
For a walk to the city.

"I've been wanting to go
To the bookstore out there,
To buy a new book
Called, *Mitzvos to Share*."

Ima agreed. "That's a great thing to do!
Why don't you see if a friend will come, too?"
Rina ran to call Bina, her very best friend,
Who lived down the path at the woods' other end.

"Bina, it's Rina; I'm calling to see
If I walk to the city, would you come with me?"

Bina said, "Yes, I'd be so pleased to spend
This lovely spring day with my very best friend!"

They decided to meet in an hour or so
And when Rina hung up, she got ready to go.
She opened the door, her purse in one hand,
Excited about the long walk she had planned.

But stepping outside, she saw right away
Clouds had covered the sun, and the sky was dark gray.
As Rina turned back, it started to pour,
So she ran straight inside and closed her front door.

It was too wet to walk now because of the rain,
But Rina was thinking and didn't complain.
**"Gam zu l'tova, I trust this is good,
Hashem makes things happen the way that they should."**

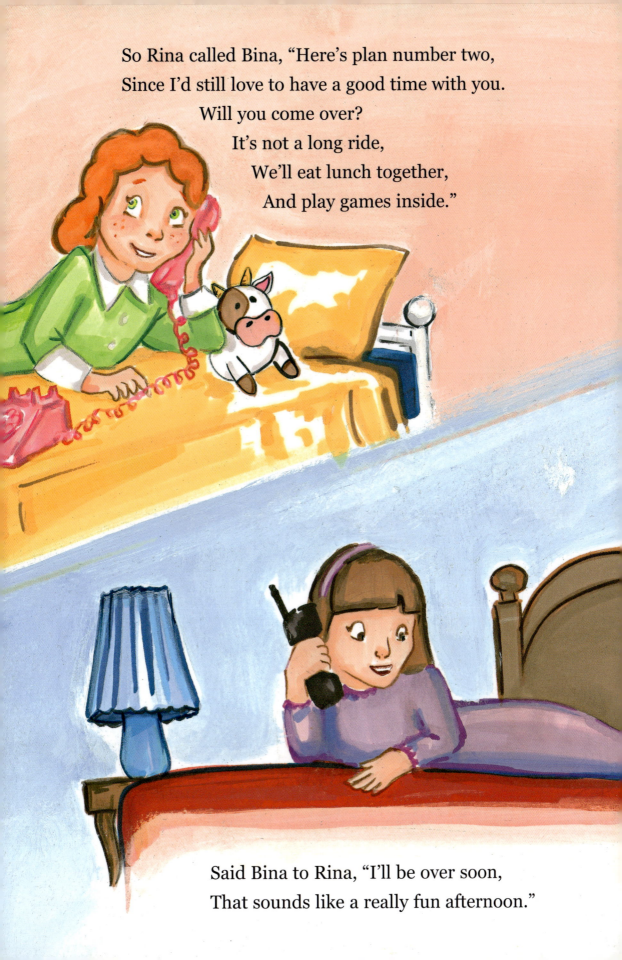

So Rina called Bina, "Here's plan number two,
Since I'd still love to have a good time with you.
Will you come over?
It's not a long ride,
We'll eat lunch together,
And play games inside."

Said Bina to Rina, "I'll be over soon,
That sounds like a really fun afternoon."

So Ima and Rina began to prepare
Soup and spaghetti for two girls to share.

They worked very hard making fresh apple pie,
Then Rina sat down with a satisfied sigh.

Just then Bina called and had something to say,
"I'm sorry, dear Rina, I can't come today.
Our car won't start up; I can't walk in this weather,
I guess that today we just can't get together."

Rina hung up, and sadly she looked
At the table she'd set and the food that she'd cooked.

"Gam zu l'tova,
I trust this is good,
Hashem makes things
happen – the way that
they should."

Then from the kitchen,
A startling sound
Made Rina jump
And look all around.

The smoke alarm rang
As loud as could be,
In a kitchen so smoky,
It grew hard to see.

She cried, "It's the pie I've forgotten about,
In the oven too long when it should have come out!"

Rina opened the window to
clear out the smoke,

Put the pie in the garbage,
and that's when she spoke:

"Gam zu l'tova,
I trust this is good,
Hashem makes things
happen – the way that
they should."

Then Rina heard knocking; she hurried to see
Who her mystery guest might turn out to be.

There stood a lady, all drenched through and through,
Her body was shaking; her lips had turned blue.

Ima brought her a bathrobe so cozy and thick,
And Rina made tea so she wouldn't get sick.
When the lady dried off from the dripping, wet rain,
She thanked them and opened her mouth to explain.

"My name's Mrs. Stein, and what I like to do
Is walk through the woods while enjoying the view.

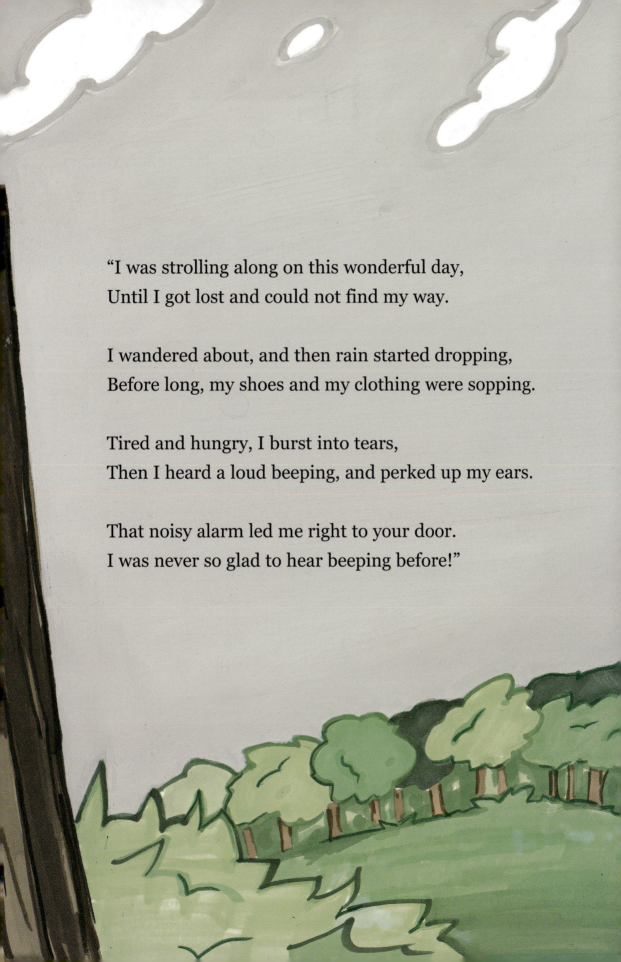

"I was strolling along on this wonderful day,
Until I got lost and could not find my way.

I wandered about, and then rain started dropping,
Before long, my shoes and my clothing were sopping.

Tired and hungry, I burst into tears,
Then I heard a loud beeping, and perked up my ears.

That noisy alarm led me right to your door.
I was never so glad to hear beeping before!"

Said Rina, "We're happy you're here as our guest,
Please join us for lunch, and take a long rest.
We're serving fresh soup and lots of spaghetti
It's really amazing that all this food's ready!

"Just when you're so tired and so hungry, too
This beautiful meal is waiting for you!
I'm anxious to tell you about my strange day,
And how each thing that happened worked out the right way:

"When my plan to go shopping came to an end,

"I stayed home to cook a nice lunch for my friend.

Mrs. Stein was so thankful, so what did she do?
She gave Rina a gift and said, "This is for you!

"I bought two new books, one for me and a spare,
So please take this one called, *Mitzvos to Share*."

Rina couldn't believe it; her plans all fell through,
And in spite of it all, her wish had come true!

Rina said, "This has been the kind of a day
That shows why it always makes sense to say,

"Gam zu l'tova, I trust this is good,
Hashem makes things happen the way that they should."